SNOWIE ROLIE

by
William Joyce

ATHENEUM
Books for Young Readers
New York London Toronto Sydney New Delhi

Rolie Polie Olie lived in a land where it never snowed. He often wished for the wonders a snowy day could bring.

Then one bright morning, the sun that shone on Olie's world blew a bulb . . .

and it started to snow!

As the world
grew white all around,
Olie and Zowie began
to build a friend . . .

named Mr. Snowie!

Oh, what fun it was with Snowie to ride on their sleigh!

But the sun got a brand-new bulb, so the world became warm and the snow became melty.

What to do? What to do? They had
a friend they couldn't keep cool!

So they took a worthy risk and rocketed to Chillsville with the AC on full blast.

The snowcapped mountains showed them the way.

But the north wind
tried to eat them up.

And down they
crashed . . .

to a place they'd heard of only in stories.

"Welcome to Chillsville," said Klanky Klaus.
"You must be hungry from your travels."

They feasted on snowdrop soup, icicle cake, and sky-high snowball pie.

And after that, they danced a chilly cha-cha . . .

all the way to Mr. Snowie's
cool new house.

We'll miss you, Mr. Snowie," said Zowie.

"But you'll be safe from now on," said Olie.

It was oh so hard
to say good-bye.

We wished for snow and we got a new friend," said Olie.

"I wish we could stay together," sighed Zowie as they rocketed away.

The journey home
was swift and sure.
Soon sleep came,
and snowy dreams
helped smiles return.

By morning, the snow was almost gone, and where Snowie once stood, there was a present . . .

a happy reminder
of their faraway friend.

Happy, sad, and everything in between—
what wonders a single snowy day can bring!

For my
faraway
friends

Super-special thanks
to the hardest-working man
in Robot Land, Jordan Thistlewood.
Also thanks to Susie Grondin, Shannon
Gilley, Gavin Boyle, Ian MacLeod, and
Ms. Lehn, the El Pammo Supreme-o, and the
Nelvana 3D production group for the reuse
of their models. And finally, thanks to
Alicia Mikles and Ruiko Tokunga,
twin Valkyries of Pixelation.

A
atheneum

ATHENEUM BOOKS FOR YOUNG READERS

An imprint of Simon & Schuster Children's Publishing
Division 1230 Avenue of the Americas, New York, New York 10020
Text copyright © 2000 by William Joyce • Illustrations copyright ©
2000 by Nelvana Limited. All rights reserved. Reprinted by permission. •
Originally published in 2000 by Laura Geringer Books/HarperCollins Publishers.
• All rights reserved, including the right of reproduction in whole or in part in any
form. • ATHENEUM BOOKS FOR YOUNG READERS is a registered trademark of Simon & Schuster,
Inc. Atheneum logo is a trademark of Simon & Schuster, Inc. • For information about special
discounts for bulk purchases, please contact Simon & Schuster Special Sales at 1-866-506-1949 or
business@simonandschuster.com.
The Simon & Schuster Speakers Bureau can bring authors to your live event.
For more information or to book an event, contact the Simon & Schuster Speakers Bureau
at 1-866-248-3049 or visit our website at www.simonspeakers.com.
Book design by Alicia Mikles • The text for this book was set in Rollie Suburban.
The illustrations for this book were digitally rendered. • Manufactured in China
0817 SCP • First Atheneum Books for Young Readers Edition
2 4 6 8 10 9 7 5 3 1
CIP data for this book is available from the Library of Congress.
ISBN 978-1-4814-8767-6
ISBN 978-1-4814-8768-3 (eBook)